MARTY FRYE PRIVATE EYE

THE CASE OF THE BUSTED VIDEO GAMES

& OTHER MYSTERIES

BOOK THREE

OUT OF ORDER

MARTY
PRIVATE EYE

FRYE
THE CASE OF THE BUSTED VIDEO GAMES
& OTHER MYSTERIES

JANET TASHJIAN
illustrated by **LAURIE KELLER**

Christy Ottaviano Books
Henry Holt and Company • New York

Henry Holt and Company
Publishers since 1866
175 Fifth Avenue,
New York, New York 10010
mackids.com

Library of Congress Cataloging-in-Publication Data

Names: Tashjian, Janet, author. | Keller, Laurie, illustrator.
Title: Marty Frye, private eye: the case of the busted video games / Janet Tashjian ;
    illustrated by Laurie Keller.
Other titles: Case of the busted video games
Description: First edition. | New York : Christy Ottaviano Books, Henry Holt and Company,
    2019. | "Book Three." | Summary: Seven-year-old Marty Frye, the poet detective, solves
    mysteries for his gym teacher, at a video arcade, and for his family.
Identifiers: LCCN 2017042625 | ISBN 9781627794619 (hardcover)
Subjects: | CYAC: Mystery and detective stories. | Vandalism—Fiction. | Lost and found
    possessions—Fiction.
Classification: LCC PZ7.T211135 Mat 2018 | DDC [Fic]—dc23
LC record available at https://lccn.loc.gov/2017042625

Our books may be purchased in bulk for promotional,
educational, or business use. Please contact your local bookseller
or the Macmillan Corporate and Premium Sales Department
at (800) 221-7945 ext. 5442 or by e-mail at
MacmillanSpecialMarkets@macmillan.com.

First edition, 2018 / Designed by April Ward and Sophie Erb

Printed in the United States of America by LSC Communications, Crawfordsville, Indiana

1 3 5 7 9 10 8 6 4 2

For Jake

—J.T.

To Super Reader (and one of
Marty's biggest fans) Sylvie Malk

—L.K.

CONTENTS

THE CASE OF THE P.E. VANDAL

THE CRIME

Marty Frye had been looking forward to gym class since he got to school. He liked Mr. Lynch, the P.E. teacher. Not just because Mr. Lynch had two pugs named Tweedle Dee and Tweedle Dum, but because Mr. Lynch knew Marty loved to climb. He let Marty scale the ropes and bleachers in the gym, and also let Marty climb the elm in the schoolyard when P.E. class was held outside. The tree wasn't as challenging as the giant maple on Marty's front lawn but it certainly was a treat to be able to scramble up the branches during school hours.

Marty just hoped there was enough time after today's jump-rope challenge to climb his beloved tree.

When Marty got to the gym after lunch, he and his classmates were in for a surprise.

It looks like we're not having our jump-rope challenge.

Several students groaned, especially Marty's friend Emma. She loved jumping rope as much as Marty loved climbing trees.

3

"Why not?" Emma asked their teacher.

Mr. Lynch dragged over a large plastic tub full of jump ropes. Each one was tied up in knots.

"We have a slight equipment problem," Mr. Lynch said. "It looks like there's a prankster in our midst."

Marty's ears perked up. He didn't care about missing the jump-rope challenge. But he DID care that Mr. Lynch was in need of a detective.

Marty waited until the rest of the class was outside before approaching Mr. Lynch.

Someone needs to connect the dots. I'LL find out who tied those knots.

Mr. Lynch stared at the jumble of jump ropes in the bin. "I *would* like to know who's behind this. So many kids were looking forward to this week's challenge."

It was Mr. Lynch's lucky day—it's not often that a teacher is fortunate enough to have a poet detective in class.

SEARCHING FOR CLUES

While his classmates ran relay races, Marty went back to his locker to get his backpack. He took out his magnifying glass and detective notebook. Whoever tampered with Mr. Lynch's gym equipment had hopefully left behind some clues.

Marty examined the two dozen jump ropes in the bin. Some were tied with one knot; others had two or three. Some of the knots were messy and some were tight and complex. Could more than one person be involved?

He knew a thorough detective would check out the rest of the gym, so Marty snooped around the basketball nets. (Those ropes were fine.)

He looked underneath all the orange cones. (He found some dried-up gum.)

He ran up and down the bleachers. (Not because they were suspicious but because it was fun.)

Emma headed in from the schoolyard to check on Marty's progress.

"I could have won the jump-rope challenge," she said. "Maybe whoever did this was afraid of losing."

Marty wrote down Emma's theory, along with a few of his own.

"It's terrible," Emma continued. "I've been practicing for weeks."

Don't give up hope—
you can still jump rope.

When Emma asked if she could tag along, Marty said yes. Solving a crime was always more fun with a friend.

Emma led Marty out to the schoolyard.

Ava has been taunting me all week about the jump-rope challenge. I bet she had something to do with this.

10

Marty ran his fingers through his hair like a comb. With Ava's long, dark braids and bright green eyes, she was the prettiest girl in school. Marty had never even talked to Ava before, and now he was supposed to question her?

He hoped his breath didn't still smell like the tuna fish sandwich he had for lunch.

I guess we won't find out if you're the school champ in the jump-rope challenge. But I'm *sure* you would've won.

The gaggle of girls around Ava laughed at her joke. Emma stood her ground.

"This is Marty—he's helping Mr. Lynch find out who sabotaged the equipment." Emma gave Marty a nudge toward Ava.

Marty cleared his throat and tried not to be mesmerized by Ava's emerald eyes. He wanted to question her but all the rhymes were caught in his throat and wouldn't come out.

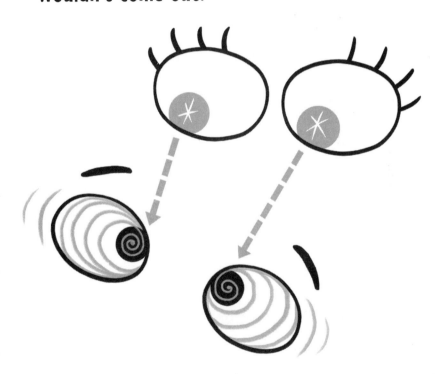

"Marty!" Emma said.

All he could do was stammer. The group of girls giggled again. The pressure was on.

"She's not a witness," Emma said. "She's a suspect!" Emma looked annoyed, which made Ava and her friends laugh even more. Emma dragged Marty away from the group.

"What was *that* about?" Emma asked Marty.

"Her eyes were so green, I forgot my routine."

Emma shook her head. "You're on your own, Marty."

With Emma gone, Marty turned to his trusty notebook. There was someone else he wanted to question: Billy Gately. Whenever there was a school prank, Billy was never far behind. Marty also knew no one had more excuses to skip P.E. than Billy. Could he have damaged

Mr. Lynch's equipment because he didn't like gym class?

Marty watched Billy against the fence with Tony. Marty and Tony had been good friends in kindergarten but hadn't done much together since Tony moved away from the neighborhood.

Marty hid behind the jungle gym to eavesdrop on their conversation. (Eavesdropping was

a very important detective skill.) But all they were talking about was Tony's upcoming Cub Scout meeting.

After Tony left, Marty came out of his hiding spot to question Billy. He tried to be a little more assertive than he had been with Ava.

He told Billy about Mr. Lynch's predicament. "Does he have you to thank for that little prank?"

Billy's ears turned red. "How come as soon as something bad happens around here, I'm the first one questioned?"

Marty listed off more than a dozen pranks Billy had played in the past year.

Billy's expression went from angry to proud. "Wow! I've been busy." His smile turned to a smirk. "I bet Mr. Lynch spends the whole afternoon untying those knots. He deserves it after all those laps he made me run yesterday."

Even though Billy denied vandalizing the equipment, Marty wasn't sure he believed him.

Emma dodged the kids playing hop-scotch and approached Marty again. "I still think Ava's behind this. She bet half the class I wouldn't win the jump-rope challenge today. Turns out she was right."

Even someone who *wasn't* a detective could tell that Emma had a problem with Ava.

"She thinks she's so perfect all the time," Emma continued.

Just because she's conceited doesn't mean she cheated.

Marty headed back inside the gym. If he was going to question Ava again, he wanted to get his facts straight.

THE SEARCH CONTINUES

It was time to revisit the scene of the crime.

Back in his office, Mr. Lynch was sitting at his desk with the jumble of ropes at his feet.

They're still in a tangle, but I need a new angle.

"Go ahead and look," the gym teacher said. "I'm not sure you're going to find anything." Mr. Lynch blew his nose. "It's a good thing I found this bandana on my desk—my allergies are bad today."

The only thing that Marty was allergic to was a crime that couldn't be solved.

He sat down by Mr. Lynch's desk and examined each jump rope one by one.

Some of the knots looped left to right; others crossed from top to bottom. A few of them were braided so tightly Marty couldn't undo them.

He threw up his hands in frustration.

I feel like a dope—
I can't fix this rope!

Mr. Lynch told Marty not to worry, that he'd take the ropes home and straighten them out. When the teacher sneezed again, Marty noticed the gold-and-blue design of his handkerchief.

Did you just say you found that today?

Mr. Lynch
nodded between
sneezes. "Some kid
must have left it. I've
never seen it before."

Marty had an idea where the fancy
bandana might have come from. He also
had an inkling who'd tied Mr. Lynch's
ropes in knots.

Marty would have to hurry; P.E. class was almost over. He gazed at the elm with its branches swaying in the breeze. Would he have time to solve this case AND go for a climb?

"Hey, Marty!" Emma called from the swings. "Do you finally have some questions for Ava?"

But Marty didn't want to question Ava. Or Billy. He looked around the schoolyard until he saw Tony.

Tony stopped in his tracks. "What do you want to know?"

Marty asked Tony if he was trying to earn a new merit badge.

Tony mumbled something about his den facing a big test.

I'll know if you're lying— is it knots that you're tying?

Tony looked around to make sure no one else was listening. "I'm the worst Cub Scout in the den! I'm the only reason we haven't earned our Bear badge. I've been practicing on every rope I can find." Tony pulled a loop of clothesline from his

backpack. "I came in early this morning to practice on this but then I saw that huge tub of ropes in the gym and got carried away."

Marty told Tony that Mr. Lynch had to cancel the school's jump-rope challenge because the ropes couldn't be used.

"I'm sorry about the challenge," Tony said. "But the good news is all that practice paid off. I'm definitely going to pass the knot-tying test in my pack tonight."

Marty followed Tony to Mr. Lynch's

office. He was glad Tony had improved his knotting skills. Marty was even glad he'd gotten out of jumping rope today. But most of all he was glad he'd solved another case.

A JOB WELL DONE

Emma kicked a clump of grass on the side of the schoolyard. "I can't believe it wasn't Ava."

You should make amends and try to be friends.

They watched Tony sitting at one of the lunch tables with the giant tub of jump ropes.

"That's going to take him hours," Emma said.

Even if it takes all day, bad guys have to pay.

A smile spread across Emma's face.

Maybe we can have the jump-rope challenge tomorrow! Maybe I can win the trophy after all.

Marty smiled too. Emma's enthusiasm was always contagious.

He watched Emma approach Tony to help him prepare the ropes for tomorrow. Marty was happy to help them, but there was something he needed to do first.

Marty shouted to his friends as he ran toward the tree.

I solved the crime; now it's time to climb!

There was nothing more satisfying than a well-deserved reward.

THE CASE OF THE BUSTED VIDEO GAMES

THE CRIME

On the drive home from school, Marty told his mother how he helped Mr. Lynch solve the P.E. mystery during gym class. His mom wanted to know all the details. (If she weren't a teacher, she would have made a good detective too.)

But Marty's little sister, Katie, didn't want to hear about his case. All Katie wanted to talk about was the new bookstore opening at the mall.

No one appreciated a good bookstore like Marty, but after a long day of solving crime he couldn't wait to get home. His mom also wanted to see the new store, so Marty had no choice but to tag along.

As they walked through the large set of doors, Marty heard shouting.

It seems there's a brawl in the middle of the mall.

Marty asked his mother if they could see what the commotion was about.

Several people were gathered outside the vintage video arcade, where Murray, the owner, was pacing back and forth, dragging his two-year-old daughter by the hand.

"Somebody's vandalizing my arcade!" the owner said. "Five of my machines are broken!"

Marty's mom and sister went ahead to the bookstore. They knew Marty would have to stay and check out the case.

SEARCHING FOR CLUES

Murray showed Marty inside. For the second time that day, Marty took out his detective notebook.

He checked out the Skee-Ball game, the karaoke machine, the race cars, and the basketball game. He looked at the snack bar with its soda, popcorn, and candy. The arcade was certainly a fun place to hang out while the rest of your family was shopping.

Marty asked the owner if he could play a few of the video games—for research.

He played Pac-Man, Frogger, and Mario before getting back to work.

Marty took out his magnifying glass
and examined the five broken games. On
each of them, a layer of goop covered the
coin slots.

Marty took a cotton swab out of his
detective kit and tried to gather evidence.
But the goop was dry and wouldn't budge.

It's a definite crime—
look at this slime.

The owner hung **OUT OF ORDER** signs on
the games. "I'm going to lose a lot of money
if this keeps up. I'll take all the help I can
get—even if it's from a second grader."

Marty tried not to be insulted. What did his age have to do with anything? He'd already solved one crime today—surely he could solve another before it was time for his afternoon snack.

He took a look around the arcade. He recognized several kids from school and a few others from the neighborhood.

Underneath the **OUT OF ORDER** sign, the name of the highest scorer was frozen on the screen.

CHANDA333

He spotted Chanda at another machine. Could she have broken these machines to retain her high score?

If anyone could figure it out, it was Marty Frye, Private Eye.

From the looks of the crowd around Chanda at the console, she was a top scorer on the *Star Wars* video game too.

When you're done with your session, can I ask you a question?

43

Chanda grinned as the kids around her cheered her on. Marty couldn't believe how many points she was racking up.

"You're the kid who rhymes all the time, right?" Chanda asked. "What do you want to know?"

It's hard to ignore that you have the high score.

Are you on a mission to destroy the competition?

When Chanda finished the game, Marty brought her over to the broken machines.

"Just because no one else can play these games now doesn't mean I'm the one who broke them," Chanda said. "I LIKE competition—it's no fun to beat everyone all the time."

Marty looked at her suspiciously.

"Okay," Chanda said. "It IS fun winning all the time. But that's not a crime, is it?"

Marty wanted to ask Chanda a few more questions, but a boy near the air hockey table caught his attention. The boy was laughing as he jammed several old prize tickets into the slots of the air hockey machine.

When Marty removed the tickets,
the boy knocked them out of his hand.

Marty recognized the boy from school.
His name was Wally and he was six
inches taller than Marty.

Wally leaned closer to Marty as he spoke. "Why do you care? Do you work here now?"

I'm here on a case— get out of my face.

Murray pulled Marty aside. He balanced his squirmy toddler on his hip.

"Another machine is broken! If this keeps up, I'll have to close the arcade."

Before I'm through,
I'll have an answer for you.

Murray told Marty he had until the end of the day before he would be forced to close.

Hopefully that would be enough time for Marty to solve the case.

Marty hid behind the karaoke machine to watch two teenage girls singing show tunes. (They weren't suspects—he just wanted to hear them. Their voices were **BAD.**) From his perch, he noticed a woman in a large woolen overcoat hanging out between two of the broken machines.

He confronted the woman and pointed to her heavy coat. "It's warm outside—what are you trying to hide?"

The woman ran for the door but Marty caught her.

"What's going on here?" Murray asked.
The woman took a bag of popcorn
from the inside of her coat. "I know
you're not supposed to bring your own
food into the arcade, but I can't afford
to buy your popcorn." The woman handed
the bag to the owner. "I'm sorry I brought
this from home."

If THIS woman didn't sabotage the machines, Marty thought, then the vandal was still at large.

Murray gave the bag of popcorn back to the woman and offered her a seat next to the karaoke machine. He then chased after his daughter, who was stumbling through the arcade.

"I remember when my kids were that young. All they did was knock things over— the house always looked like a tornado hit it!"

The woman's eyes filled with happy tears at the memory.

Marty watched the little girl careen down the aisle, spilling her juice all over the floor. He turned to the woman eating her popcorn.

Please don't get teary— you gave me a theory!

He ran to tell the owner he'd just cracked the case.

Marty ran by Chanda sitting in one of the race cars.

"Hey, Mr. Detective—want to race?" Chanda asked.

I'm in a hurry— I've got to find Murray!

He found the owner wiping a puddle of his daughter's drink from the floor.

This isn't a maybe—
the culprit's your baby!

Marty brought Murray over to the row
of broken machines and pointed to the slots.
"If I had to deduce, I'd say this was juice."

Murray watched his daughter bounce
between the machines—at the same height
as the coin slots. "I thought someone was
damaging my machines on purpose," Murray
said. "I can't believe the answer was under

my nose the whole time. This is all my fault—I never should've mixed fruit with yogurt, chocolate milk, and ice cream!"

That crazy brew turned into glue.

The woman with the popcorn reassured Murray. "How were you to know you'd need a pro?" She shot Marty a wink. "You're not the only one who can rhyme."

The woman crumpled the empty bag of popcorn into a ball, hopped on her toes, and aimed. The makeshift ball landed squarely in the wastebasket on the other side of the room.

A smile spread across Marty's face and he pulled out a quarter from his pocket.

My work is done—let's have some fun.

Murray, his daughter, and the lady with the popcorn followed Marty to the karaoke machine.

A JOB WELL DONE

When Marty's mom and sister returned from the bookstore, Marty was singing the theme song from *The Banana Splits* show with Chanda and Wally. Murray grabbed the juice cup away from the baby just as she was about to spill it all over the karaoke machine.

"That girl is a menace!" Wally said.

Marty defended Murray's daughter.

58

> You can't blame a kid—
> that cup needs a lid!

Murray said he would make his daughter a healthier drink tomorrow.

"You ready to go?" Marty's mom asked. "I've got dinner to prepare and papers to grade."

Marty and his sister followed their mom to the parking garage.

"Wait!" Murray hurried to catch up. He handed Marty a string of prize tickets. "Next time, I promise not to make you work. Just come and play."

No one had to ask Marty twice to play video games at the arcade. He told Murray he'd see him soon.

THE CASE OF THE MISSING PHONE

THE CRIME

Marty and Katie put the groceries away while their mom roasted a chicken for dinner. Their cat, Rip Van Winkle, rubbed against Katie's leg.

"I guess you're hungry." Katie opened a can of food and dumped it into Rip Van Winkle's bowl.

"While you're at it, can someone clean Mr. Van Winkle's litter box?" their mom asked.

Marty and Katie played Rock, Paper, Scissors to decide which of them would get stuck with the dreaded job. Marty cheered when his scissors beat Katie's paper. She shuffled off to the basement to empty the cat's litter box.

I solved two cases today— hip, hip, hooray! Marty thought as he went upstairs. Hopefully he'd have as much success with tonight's science homework.

He'd read only a few pages before his mother came upstairs and asked Marty if he'd seen her phone.

"I thought I put it on the kitchen table when we came back from the mall," she said. "But I've looked everywhere and can't find it."

She tilted her head and looked at her son. "I might have to hire a private detective. Do you know where I can find a good one?"

Marty closed his textbook.

With your permission, can I apply for the position?

"The job is yours," his mom said. "See if you can find it before dinner."

It was a challenge Marty was happy to accept.

If Marty's calculations were correct, his mother had misplaced her phone fifty million times this year. He asked if she'd checked her purse, her car, and the table by the door where she always put her keys.

"I've looked in all the usual places," she said. "But this time I really think it's gone."

Don't you fret— we'll find it yet.

Marty took out his magnifying glass and checked inside the fridge between the cartons of milk and juice. He checked the oven. (Potatoes and chicken were all he found.) He took everything out of his mom's purse—what a mess!—then put it all back when he didn't find the phone.

"I called my cell from the home phone," his mom said. "But I didn't hear it ring. I don't think it's in the house."

It was time for some real private-eye work. Marty called the manager of the bookstore and Murray at the video arcade to see if his mother had left her phone at the mall. Neither of them had seen it.

Next, Marty tracked down Katie playing with her dolls on the porch. The dolls were dressed in their best clothes and Katie was spraying them with her mother's perfume.

"Don't they look nice?" Katie asked. "They're on their way to a dance."

Marty rolled his eyes. How could Katie play while a mystery was unfolding right before their eyes?

Put down that cologne—Mom lost her phone.

He asked Katie if she'd seen the phone since they returned from the mall.

Katie took the scarf off one doll and put it on another. "Maybe Joel saw it. He's out back."

Joel was the handyman who sometimes helped their mother with tasks around the house.

"His nephew is with him today," Katie continued. "You can ask him too."

Marty was already on his way outside.

Joel was in the backyard replacing a fuse in the electrical panel while his nephew, Luke, sat on the lawn playing a game—the same game Marty's mom often played on HER phone. Marty wondered if Luke had borrowed his mom's phone to entertain himself while his uncle

I'm not here to blame, but is that my mom's game?

worked. He sat on the grass next to Luke. Luke barely looked up from the screen. "I discovered this app when I found the phone. It's really fun."

This was perhaps the easiest case Marty had ever solved. He told Luke he was glad he liked playing the game but it was time to return the phone to his mother.

"No!" Luke said. "I found this phone fair and square."

Joel closed the electrical panel and asked Marty what was going on. Marty explained that Luke had borrowed his mother's phone without her permission.

I don't mean to attack, but my mom needs it back.

Marty held out his hand for Luke to return the phone.

Luke only clenched it tighter.

"I'm confused, Luke," Joel said. "I thought that was your phone."

It is!

Marty asked Luke where he found it. Perhaps on their kitchen table?

"I'm not telling," Luke said. "And I'm NOT giving it back."

Luke jumped over the hedge and out of the yard.

Joel shook his head and turned to Marty. "Luke's having a hard time at school. Don't worry—I'll get to the bottom of this," he said.

Marty appreciated that Joel was trying to help. But didn't he understand that getting to the bottom of things was MARTY'S job?

Marty looked down the street for Luke. He looked in the garage.

He looked in his favorite tree. Would he have time for two climbs in one day?

But what if Luke **WASN'T** the thief? Marty didn't want to waste valuable time if someone else was responsible for taking his mom's phone. He decided to ask Jackie, their next-door neighbor, if she'd seen anything suspicious.

Jackie was in her backyard wearing a jumpsuit and a beekeeper's helmet.

She lifted her veil and ran over to Marty. "I'm so glad you're here. I'm hunting for bees—help me find some!"

Every time Marty saw Jackie she was doing something original (and kind of weird).

I hate to displease, but I can't look for bees.

He asked Jackie if she happened to see his mom's missing phone.

"I talked to Katie a little while ago," Jackie said. "She didn't mention anything about your mom's lost phone."

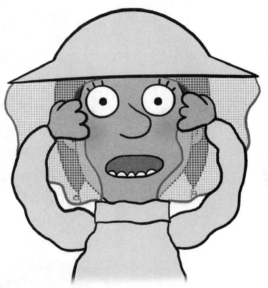

Marty asked Jackie if he could examine her phone. He looked at the number of the last call that came in. Sure enough, his hunch was right. "I know this number well—Katie called from Mom's cell."

He now had an idea what had happened to his mother's phone. He told Jackie he had to go.

"Hey! What about the bees?" Jackie called after him.

I've got to set something straight— finding bees will have to wait.

Marty ran the whole way home.

AHA!

Katie was on the porch, making her dolls dance around Rip Van Winkle. The cat did not seem amused by the festivities. Marty confronted his sister.

When you were alone, you used Mom's phone.

Katie turned down the music so she could hear her brother. "What are you talking about?" Katie asked. "I've been here since we got back from the mall."

Marty realized his mistake. He'd retraced his mother's steps this afternoon but hadn't retraced Katie's.

He guided his sister through their afternoon.

First putting away the groceries.

Then feeding the cat.

Then Rock, Paper, Scissors.

Then emptying the litter box.

Katie's hand flew to her mouth. "Now I remember!"

Marty led Katie to the basement. They bent down to the litter box next to the sink as Rip Van Winkle looked on with disapproval.

Marty ran to his room to get his detective kit and then slipped on a pair of latex gloves. (Evidence had to be protected. So did his hands since cat poop was involved.)

He carefully rummaged through the box until he felt a small rectangle buried in the fresh litter. Marty pulled out his mom's phone.

In your haste to empty the waste, might I ask if you multi-tasked?

Even climbing their maple tree was not as gratifying as a quadruple rhyme. He was nailing his rhymes **AND** his crimes today.

"I forgot that I used Mom's phone to call Jackie while I was down here," Katie said. "I must've dropped it when I replaced the litter."

Marty brushed the fresh litter off the phone and handed it to Katie.

I'm sure Mom won't be sore since you completed your chore.

Katie returned the phone to her mom just as she was taking the chicken out of the oven. Their mom was very happy to have her cell phone back.

"And you beat the dinner deadline," Mom said. "Nice job, Marty."

Even Marty had to admit he'd been an awfully good detective today.

A JOB WELL DONE

Joel marched his nephew into the Fryes' kitchen. Luke stared down at his feet as he spoke.

"I'm sorry I was rude," Luke said. "But I found this phone in the woods, not here."

"We went through the recent calls and located the phone's owner," Joel said.

Joel told his nephew that the woman who lost her phone had been looking for it all day.

"Too bad she doesn't have a detective in the family like I do," Mrs. Frye said.

"But in a weird way, Marty helped that woman get her phone back too," Joel said. "I never would've known it was lost if Marty hadn't asked Luke about it. We're on our way to return it now."

Marty was glad he'd been able to help someone else too, but when he glanced at Luke, he seemed sad. Marty took his mom's phone off the counter and handed it to Luke.

No need for blame—
want to finish your game?

Luke's face lit up as he grabbed the phone, eager to open the app.

"Joel, how about a plate of chicken and veggies before you and Luke go?" Marty's mom asked.

She didn't have to ask twice.

As everyone served themselves, Katie snuck up behind her brother.

Hey! Marty thought.
First the popcorn lady, now
my sister? Rhyming is MY routine! But the
kitchen was full of delicious food and
friends, so he decided not to complain.

He beat Katie to the counter and handed her a plate.

Katie, maybe it's time WE ALL talked in rhyme!

"Don't get used to it," Katie said. "It was a one-time thing."

That was okay with Marty. Having one poet detective in the family was probably enough.

That night in bed, Marty reviewed his notes from the day. Three crimes, plenty of rhymes, and two tree-climbing sessions. (After-dinner climbs were the absolute best.)

He shut off the light and put his notebook on the nightstand. If he was lucky, tomorrow might be another great day.